KATIE'S KINGFISHER

and

other women's magazine stories

MARGARET KAINE

COLLEYWOOD PRESS

ISBN: 978-0-9575108-2-1

All of the following short stories have previously been published in various women's magazines. Why not enjoy a distraction from everyday life, have coffee and cake, a glass of wine or dip into a box of chocolates.

Contents

KATIE'S KINGFISHER   5

WHEN THE CHIPS ARE DOWN   10

LITTLE IN COMMON   15

NICOLA   20

A FRIENDSHIP SPLIT   24

A PERSONAL CHOICE   29

KINDRED SPIRITS   35

NOTHING TO PROVE   39

DRIVING MRS MURPHY   43

A FATEFUL MEETING   47

Contents

KATIE'S KINGFISHER

Mary leaned against the cool stone of the ancient hump-backed bridge, hoping that she hadn't been mistaken. Then she caught her breath at the sheer beauty of the graceful bird poised on the weeping willow which bent its branches down to the water.

It was years since she'd seen a kingfisher and she remained still, wanting to hold the moment, to capture the peace and tranquillity of the age-old setting. A few hundred yards away lay the village with its bustle and traffic, but Mary closed her mind to intrusion. She stood drinking in the glory of the bird's brilliant blue-green plumage.

She was so lost in her reverie, she was startled when a small figure squeezed in beside her.

'What are you looking at?'

'Ssh.' Mary pointed.

The child gave a sharp intake of breath and her lips curving in wonder, looked up at Mary with shining eyes.

'It's a kingfisher,' Mary whispered.

The bird fluttered its wings and in a flash of sapphire and rich chestnut, flew to a further branch.

Mary glanced towards the village, anxious that the little girl, who couldn't have been more than six years old, was on her own. But a woman chatting to a friend waved, and Mary relaxed.

'Magic!' the little girl murmured.

'It's very special,' Mary agreed. 'What's your name?'

'Katie,' she answered.

Mary looked down at her. She was a pale child, with large, luminous blue eyes. Mary smiled down at the top of a sun hat. Not a lock of hair peeked out, and she could only guess that she was blonde.

'You had a sad face,' Katie said suddenly.

'Sorry?' Mary said.

'Before, when you were walking up to the bridge.'

'I'm not sad really, Katie, I just have an important decision to make, and it's on my mind.' Mary was surprised to find herself confiding in one so young, but Katie's thoughtful gaze seemed wise beyond her years.

'Mum says a trouble shared is a trouble halved,' Katie offered. 'You can talk to me about it, if you like.'

Mary was bemused. What an unusual child, she thought with delight. She'd forgotten the joy children could bring. Her own two had long flown the nest. Her son lived abroad, and Teresa, her daughter, had moved away to Cork. That was part of her problem.

'Thank you, Katie. I'd like that,' she said softly.

Katie waited.

'Well,' Mary began, 'I've lived here all my life. My children went to the village school and my husband was the postman. I've never lived anywhere else.'

'I've always lived here too,' Katie said. 'I like it.'

'So do I, Katie. The trouble is, I'm getting old. You can see that by my white hair.' Mary smiled. 'I've got arthritis …'

'My granny's got that,' Katie interrupted. 'She says she needs filleting.'

Mary laughed. 'I know how she feels.'

'Are you a granny, too?'

'No, I'm afraid not.' It was a huge disappointment

to her not to have grandchildren. Although she hadn't given up hope. 'I can't manage on my own very well,' she explained. 'My daughter wants me to go to live near her, a long way away, but that would mean leaving the village.'

Katie considered. 'You wouldn't know anyone at this other place.'

'No, I wouldn't,' Mary said sadly.

'But you'd be with your daughter. Mum says family is the most important thing in the world.'

Mary smiled. 'I think your Mum is a very wise woman.'

Katie caught her arm. 'Quick, he's flying away.'

They watched enraptured as the kingfisher streaked along the level of the water, and then flew out of sight.

'You'll always remember today, Katie,' Mary said. 'Only very lucky people see kingfishers, you know.'

'Really?' Katie breathed.

'I do hope she hasn't been a nuisance.'

Mary turned as Katie's mother came hurrying up to take the little girl's hand.

'I've seen a kingfisher,' Katie said excitedly.

'Well, aren't you the lucky one. I've never seen one,' her mother admitted.

'I told you, didn't I?' Mary smiled.

'Come on, Katie, we'd better be going. Say thank you to Mrs …'

'Egan, Mary Egan.'

'Bye, Mrs Egan,' Katie waved.

'Bye, Katie. Thank you for your advice,' Mary called, wondering why had it taken a six year old child to pinpoint her priorities.

It was a few weeks later when she saw Katie's mother

again. She was leaning against the bridge, staring down into the swirling water. As Mary approached, she turned and waited.

'Do you remember me?' Mary asked. 'Katie and I watched the kingfisher together.'

'Yes, of course I do. I'm Angela Horan, by the way.'

'How's Katie? At school, I suppose. She's a most unusual and intelligent little girl. I did enjoy talking to her.'

Angela's smile seemed poignant in a way that Mary found oddly moving. 'No, she's not at school. Do you remember she was wearing a sun hat when you met her? Well, it was covering where her hair used to be …'

Mary gave a sharp cry of distress.

Angela touched her hand reassuringly. 'There's no need to worry, Katie's at home resting. The doctors are very pleased with her. They say her positive attitude has helped enormously. And you know a lot of credit for that is due to you.'

'Me?' Mary was completely mystified.

'It was the kingfisher,' Angela explained. 'Katie told me she knew she'd get better because seeing the kingfisher meant she was lucky. And if she was lucky, then how could she keep being ill?'

Mary blinked back tears.

'Oh Angela, what can I say? She helped me too, you know, helped me to make a decision. I'm leaving the village and going to live near my daughter in Cork.'

'Katie said you would,' Angela said. 'I was hoping to see you, that's why I've been coming to the bridge. She wanted you to have this.'

With a trembling hand, Mary opened the sheet of paper. The childish drawing was unmistakeable. It was a kingfisher, and underneath, so painstakingly printed in red crayon, was the simple message, 'Good Luck Mary, from Katie xxx'

~

WHEN THE CHIPS ARE DOWN

'The flaming computer's crashed again!' Trish burst angrily into the sitting room.

Andy, tousle-headed and unshaven yawned, immersed in the sports pages of the daily paper.

'You know what the trouble is, don't you? You've got a Friday afternoon job, a dud model.'

Obviously bored with the subject, he switched on the TV. Trish glared at the back of his head. He wasn't exactly supportive she thought grimly. Okay, so it was her flat, she'd bought the computer, and she could deal with it. But he might show a bit more interest in her problems. In fact, he might show more interest in anything. She'd tried reading aloud to him from her new paperback, 'Men are from Mars, Women are from Venus', in an effort to improve their relationship, but he'd soon lost interest. Sometimes she wondered whether he only came round to watch cricket and soccer on her satellite channel.

'I don't know why you had to go and buy a computer in the first place,' Andy complained.

'It's better than watching the box for hours on end,' she snapped. 'At least I'm learning something!'

He merely aimed the remote control at the TV and shrugged.

Trisha glared at the back of his head, and refusing to accept defeat, went back to the shop.

'Remember me?' she said to the young salesman.

He looked at her vaguely.

'I'm the sucker who bought a computer from you four months ago.'

Daylight dawned behind his spectacles. 'Oh yes. Is there another problem?'

'I'll say there is, and I want my money back or a replacement.' Her face nearly as red as her hair, Trish squared her shoulders, ready for battle.

'I'm afraid that's not company policy.'

'And what is?' She raised her voice. 'Selling faulty goods?'

He glanced round nervously.

'Perhaps you could just tell me ...'

She did, stressing that in the whole time she'd had the computer, she'd managed to get online exactly twice.

'And it's not user error either, even if I am a beginner. At least two friends who are computer literate have tested it out.'

But her protest was ignored as he said in a bored tone, 'If you bring it in, we're quite willing to carry out any repairs needed.'

'You've already had it back three times,' she flung at him.

He shrugged. 'Like the manager told you last time, I'm afraid there's nothing else we can do.'

Trish could have wept with frustration, but she didn't, she phoned and vented it on Andy.

'You could stop your monthly payments,' was his only suggestion.

'Oh yeah, and get my name on some credit blacklist. You're a great help!'

It took three days for Trish to come up with her master plan. Fired with enthusiasm, she told Andy.

'You wouldn't have the nerve,' he scoffed.

'Just you watch me!' She waited to see if he'd offer to come with her, but he was already immersed in his TV programme.

So, early on Saturday morning, Trish elbowed her way into the shop. 'Excuse me,' she said to a dark haired guy of her own age, who was browsing among the computers. He moved out of the way as she set up her folding canvas chair before the display, and placed a placard on her lap. It proclaimed in large red letters, 'I demand a replacement or a refund.'

'What are you doing?' The salesman was horrified.

'Staging a sit-in,' she announced. 'And I've brought my flask and sandwiches.' She turned to the young man. 'I wouldn't buy a computer from here,' she warned. 'Mine's useless!'

He began to grin. 'Now that's what I call style!' He leaned against the counter, and watched with interest. Other people began to gather round and through them pushed a grey haired man, whose badge proclaimed him the manager. His startled expression took in the situation.

'I'm afraid you can't stay there, Madam.'

Trish smiled angelically at him. 'Try and move me.'

He went into a huddle with the assistant, while Trish found she was beginning to enjoy herself.

'Good for you, love,' called a woman with peroxide hair. 'About time someone stuck up for us consumers.'

The manager began to speak to Trish as if she was a child. 'My member of staff has followed the correct procedure, Miss er …'

'Walters,' Trish said helpfully.

'Yes. I'm afraid we can only follow company policy.'

'Then change it!' she challenged.

'I'd report them to the Office of Fair Trading,' someone suggested.

The manager blanched.

Trish reached for her flask and poured out coffee, slightly disappointed to see that the dark haired guy had disappeared.

By now, the manager was looking distinctly harassed. 'We will not give in to threats!' he blustered.

'I'm only after justice,' Trish protested.

'It's a free country!' someone in the crowd shouted.

The manager leaned forward and hissed at Trish, 'You're causing a public disturbance. I'll give you ten minutes, then I'm calling the police!'

Trish began to waver, the last thing she wanted was a criminal record. But if she left, she'd have achieved nothing, just made a public exhibition of herself. She looked around the sea of faces, hoping in vain that Andy had changed his mind and come to give her moral support.

Then suddenly there came a shout, 'Hold it there!' Trish turned into the flash, to see the dark haired guy behind a camera.

'Front page stuff this,' he announced, turning as if to go.

The manager's face grew purple. 'Okay, you win,' he muttered to Trish. 'Bring it back and you can have a replacement.'

'I'm a witness to that,' the photographer warned.

Elated, Trish collected her belongings, and grinned ecstatically at him. 'How can I ever thank you?'

He smiled down at her. 'You can always buy me a drink.'

She looked up at him, really liking what she saw. This was what she needed in a boyfriend, someone to be there for her, to stand in her corner. Andy was just a waste of space. Trish glanced down at the placard, at the red letters demanding a replacement or a refund. Well, she thought, there was no way she could get a refund on all the money she'd spent on Andy. But she could certainly get a replacement boyfriend!

She smiled back at the young man before her.

'I think that's a great idea!'

LITTLE IN COMMON

Ann glared at Michael. 'You did what?' She couldn't believe he'd inflicted this on her, and at such short notice.

'It just came out,' he said lamely. 'Dermot was saying that Helen sometimes gets lonely when he's away on a trip, and I said …'

'Why doesn't she come round and have a meal with us tonight? Yes, I heard you the first time!' Ann continued stacking the breakfast dishes. 'Honestly, Michael, you do land me in it.'

'I can't see what you're making such a fuss about. One more won't make much difference.' He gave her a quick kiss, and was gone.

Ann felt like screaming. Did he think she could offer cottage pie to the superior Helen? Not only was the elegant brunette the wife of Michael's boss, she made Ann feel totally inadequate.

'Mummy!' Four year old Kieran pulled at her sleeve. 'Is it time to go yet?'

'Yes, sweetheart. I'll just put Mary in her pushchair.'

She was glad it was Kieran's morning for nursery. That would give her a couple of hours to clean the house. She had only met Helen twice. The first time had been at the firm's Christmas party. Ann had felt tongue-tied at the elegance of Helen's red cocktail dress, diamond drop-earrings and long slim legs. The second time was one Saturday when she and Michael were taking the kids to McDonald's and the two couples came face to face.

'I'm just taking Helen for a birthday lunch at The Grand,' Dermot had murmured, smiling down at the children, while Helen stood to one side looking bored.

'You remember Michael and …' Dermot began.

'Ann,' Michael supplied.

'Yes, of course.' Helen's tone was cold and to Ann, she seemed patronising. As for the children, Helen had ignored them completely.

After Ann had dropped Kieran off at nursery, nine-month old Mary decided to co-operate by falling asleep in her playpen. Ann blitzed the house frantically. Even after all her efforts, the sitting room still looked drab. Flowers, that's what she needed. Flowers always breathed life into a room. She planned her shopping. Two cartons of fresh soup, rolls, fillets of salmon, new potatoes, a lemon tart for dessert, and wine.

'Sorry, Michael,' she thought. 'It was your idea so you'll have to pay for it!'

Then at 6 o'clock, he rang to say something urgent had cropped up and he'd be late home. Ann blew her top.

'How can you do this to me!' she exploded. 'Your boss's wife is arriving soon, I look a mess, and I need you to look after Kieran and Mary while I get changed.'

'I'm sorry, I'll be there as soon as I can,' he apologised.

However, when the doorbell rang, Michael was stuck in a traffic jam and Ann was stuck in T-shirt and jeans, wiping ketchup from two small faces. Heart sinking, she shooed Kieran upstairs, scooped Mary into her arms and went to open the front door.

'Hi,' she said brightly. 'Come in, Helen.'

Helen stepped inside and silently handed Ann an

expensive bottle of wine.

'Thank you.' With an envious glance at Helen's cream designer suit, Ann forced a smile.

'Excuse the workwear, Michael's late and the children have only just finished their supper.'

'Of course,' said Helen.

The atmosphere was so strained that when Mark arrived barely ten minutes later, Ann's relief exceeded her anger, but only just.

'Michael, can you offer Helen a drink. I must get the kids to bed and then I'll change,' she said pointedly.

Fifteen minutes later she was back, wearing a blue shift dress that she knew set off her blonde hair.

The meal went much as she'd expected. The food was fine, but talking to Helen was like taking a cold shower.

'Open the bottle she brought too, for heaven's sake,' Ann whispered, as Michael carried some plates into the kitchen.

But when Ann returned with the lemon tart, Michael had disappeared and Helen was sitting alone with her full wine glass, staring out of the window.

'The baby was crying,' she explained.

'Oh,' said Karen flatly. She imagined that Helen's dinner parties all ran like clockwork, with *cordon bleu* cooking and crystal wine glasses. She glanced uncomfortably at their own, which had come free with petrol at the local garage.

'It's no use,' Michael apologised when he came back. 'Mary's woken up Kieran, and he refuses to go back to sleep until he's seen the lady and said goodnight to her, too.'

Helen looked at him. 'Do you mean me?'

'I'm afraid so,' Michael said with a cheerful grin.

Ann waited for Helen's reaction. Surely she wouldn't be able to resist little Kieran, all cuddly in his pyjamas?

'I'd rather not,' she answered coolly.

Ann and Michael looked stunned.

'He's only a little boy,' Ann said tersely. 'He won't understand.'

Helen hesitated.

'Oh, all right then.' She walked swiftly from the room.

'It's on the left,' Michael called after her.

'Did you ever!' Ann hissed. 'I'm going up. I don't want her upsetting them.'

Seething, she tiptoed upstairs, then suddenly stopped. Helen was standing next to Kieran's bed, looking down at the little boy's impish face with a look of utter longing. Ann realised with shock that she was close to tears.

'Helen, what's the matter?' Ann asked gently.

Helen turned, her coolness gone. 'I'm sorry. It's just that they're both so adorable. I do envy you, Ann.'

'You? Envy me?' Ann stared at her, bewildered.

'Everyone thinks I don't want children. But it's not that,' Helen flushed. 'I can't have any, you see. That's why I try to avoid them. It upsets me so much.'

Leaning over Mary's cot, she caressed the baby's silky hair. 'Dermot wants us to adopt, but it wouldn't be the same.'

'Wouldn't it?' Ann said softly. 'If I'd actually given birth to Kieran and Mary, do you think I could love them any more than I do?'

Puzzled, Helen stared at her for a moment. Then she smiled, a vulnerable, warm smile of hope and happiness, as Ann's gaze met hers in perfect understanding.

~

NICOLA

'What do you mean, you're not coming for Sunday lunch? You know how much Dad looks forward to seeing you, and Gran.'

Nicola winced. 'I can't face anyone. I'm sorry, Mum!'

Her mother's sympathetic, yet impatient reaction ringing in her ears, Nicola shakily replaced the receiver. How could Paul have done it, hurt her so much just one month before their wedding? Nicola wandered miserably into her small sitting room and slumped on the cream sofa. 'It's the thought of being tied down,' he'd muttered, 'having a mortgage hanging over me, kids, the whole package.'

Was that where they'd gone wrong? Too much self-denial while they saved to get married?

At work, her friends were full of sympathy but strangely, not surprised. 'We always thought he was a loser,' they admitted.

'Well, he's history!' Nicola said airily, but she turned away to hide her heartache. It was the rejection that hurt most. A month later, unable to sleep, she got up early and sipping her coffee stood staring out of the window. It was a beautiful morning; the birds were singing, and the May blossom was in bud. I'm so stupid, she thought, to let things get me down like this. But she couldn't help it – her whole life at the moment seemed lacklustre. With a sigh, she turned away to make her solitary breakfast.

Later, she forced herself to go out for a walk hoping

the fresh air would improve her mood. Then startled as a car passed at high speed, she turned to see it screech to a halt further along the road. The passenger door opened, a bundle was flung out, and then the door slammed shut as the car sped away. Nicola approached warily then seeing movement, bent and drew back the threadbare grey towel. Inside was a tiny quivering puppy. Horrified, even though the car had disappeared, Nicola yelled in fury, 'Morons!'

Seething with anger, she picked up the tiny animal and gazed down into frightened brown eyes. She held it protectively against her, wondering how anyone could be so cruel then hurried back home, where, after lapping at a bowl of rice pudding, the puppy curled up on one of Nicola's old jumpers. She stroked his soft black fur gently, watching him while he slept. The room was quiet. She couldn't bear watching other people's happiness portrayed on TV. The radio too, was full of love songs, romantic tunes. I'm finished with all that, she thought.

In the afternoon she carried the puppy outside and placed it on the lawn, looking up as Kay, her next-door neighbour called from her garden, 'Isn't it a gorgeous day? Don't forget Millie's birthday party this afternoon.'

'Look!' Nicola lifted up the puppy to show her. 'You'll never believe it, but someone threw him out of a car this morning. I found him on the pavement!'

'What!' Kay's good-natured face was appalled. 'Bring him round with you, my cousin's coming and he's a vet. I'll ask him to check it over.'

So when Nicola went round to the party, it was with the puppy clinging sleepily to her shoulder. Kay hastily introduced her to a tall, dark-haired young man. 'This is Simon,' she said, and with a quick smile he took the puppy and disappeared into the kitchen. Nicola went gingerly into the crowded sitting room. The noise was deafening, and she was trying to avoid being crashed into by a toddler pushing a truck, when Simon returned.

'What's the verdict?' She glanced at him with anxiety.

'He's perfectly healthy. I'd guess there's a bit of collie in there. Are you going to keep him?'

She cuddled the puppy in her arms. 'I'd love to, but I'm out at work all day. It wouldn't be fair.'

'I bet Kay would be only too happy to give him some company. You know how much she misses Susie.' Kay's much-loved spaniel had died six months earlier.

Nicola suddenly made a decision. 'Okay, I will.'

'So, what will you call him?'

Nicola stroked the tiny form in her arms. Maybe something to fit in with his gleaming black fur? She smiled. 'I'll have to give it some thought.'

With a tug at her sleeve, little Millie said in a loud whisper, 'Please may I hold him?'

Nicola bent down and whispered back, 'Yes, but be very careful, he's only a baby.' She passed the wriggling body over, smiling as Millie kissed the top of his head. Later, holding him again in her arms, she glanced around the room at the boisterous children. Suddenly she realised how self-centred she'd been, shutting herself away, giving no thought to others. But not as selfish as those callous people! The poor little thing could have crawled into the road, been run over, or even broken a leg! Didn't they know there were Animal Rescue Shelters? Then glancing round, she saw the wistful expression on Kay's unguarded face, and remembering Millie's delight when she'd clutched the puppy in her small arms, Nicola felt a pang of guilt. She hesitated, then began to weave her way across the room.

Later, when the party was over, Simon came over. He was smiling. 'Little Millie's thrilled to bits with her new pet and so is Kay. They're busy thinking of names. That's going to be one very spoiled little dog.' He hesitated. 'I wondered Nicola whether you'd like to come out for dinner with me? Perhaps one day this week?

Nicola guessed that Kay would have told him about Paul, but suddenly she didn't mind any more about people knowing. And it had taken caring for a defenceless puppy to achieve that, to melt the ice in her heart. She gazed at him and smiled. 'I'd like that very much.' Could this, she thought, be her first step to a normal life again?

Later the following week when the telephone rang, Nicola smiled to herself, knowing who it would be. 'Hello, mum. Yes, of course I'll be there for Sunday lunch. Don't worry, I'm feeling much better now.'

~

A FRIENDSHIP SPLIT

*Forgiveness is the key to happiness, for
without it there is no inner peace.*

Hannah stared at the sentence in the self-help book
she'd found at a church bazaar. Well, she could certainly
identify with that. The only problem was that it could
be too late for herself and Cathy.

With an anxious frown, Hannah put the last touch
to her make-up and then paused. Should she? Did she
really want to take the risk? She could go down today,
this morning even, in this glorious summer weather.

Forgiveness was such an emotive word. The problem
was that not only did it have to be offered, it had to be
accepted too. Given the circumstances, was it possible
for either of those things to happen?

Hannah was still asking herself that question when
the train pulled into the small familiar station. Slowly,
in the warm sunshine, she walked along the high street.
Not much had changed in the past four years, an estate
agent where a small boutique used to be, a delicatessen
in place of a shoe-shop. "Blood sisters to the end,"
they'd sworn as they grew up together, vowing that
nothing could ever split them up. But for four years
now they hadn't seen each other and the absence of
Cathy in Hannah's life had left a hole no one else could
fill.

Turning left, she made her way to the avenue where
she and Cathy had grown up. Hannah's own parents

had retired to the coast two years ago. Pausing briefly outside her old home, she saw toys in the front garden and smiled. It was good to think of children in that house again. Cathy's parents had lived three doors away and, hoping they'd still be there and would be able to tell her Cathy's new address, Hannah opened their gate and walked slowly, her nerves tense up the path. After all, she hardly thought that she would be their favourite person. She took a deep breath and then rang the doorbell. Nobody answered. Hannah rang again and seconds later when it was opened, she stared in profound shock at the flame-haired, heavily pregnant young woman facing her. Hannah's stomach lurched, her throat closing in panic. This was something she hadn't expected, hadn't quite prepared herself for, not yet.

'Cathy! I was expecting your mother to answer,' she stammered.

'Mum and Dad have moved to a bungalow.' Cathy's voice gave no indication of her feelings. 'We bought the house from them.'

'I see,' Hannah muttered.

Cathy stood aside, her voice cool. 'You'd better come in.'

Hannah followed her into the sitting room. 'This all looks so different from how I remember it,' she said, looking at the white walls and gleaming paintwork. The windows bore pale coffee linen curtains, the neutral carpet a sea of tranquillity. Gone was the fussiness she remembered.

Cathy turned to face her. 'Thanks. But I'm sure you haven't come here to admire my decorating.'

'Please, Cathy – it's been four years.'

'I know that, Han…'

Vulnerable tears threatened at the nickname only Cathy had ever used, and Hannah turned her head away.

'Sit down,' Cathy said abruptly. 'I'll put the kettle on. Black coffee?'

Hannah nodded. She had never expected Cathy to be pregnant, it hurt not to have known that. 'When is the baby due?' she called through to the kitchen.

'Another three weeks,' Cathy called back.

Hannah, unable to sit still, wandered over to the sideboard to look at a photograph in a silver frame. Cathy looked so beautiful in her wedding dress yet Hannah, who at one time would have been chief bridesmaid, hadn't even been invited.

For the two once close friends, everything had changed from the moment Michael had entered their lives. It had happened while Hannah was away on a training course for six weeks and even now, she could remember her shock on returning to find Cathy already engaged.

'Oh, Hannah, just wait until you meet him,' Cathy's eyes had been alight with happiness, and to her dismay Hannah had felt a sharp pang of jealousy. Would this Michael come between them, affect their friendship? She'd seen it happen so many times, girls getting married and then drifting away from their friends. But surely, that couldn't possibly happen with herself and Cathy.

Then Hannah met him. He was absolutely devastating!

'Hannah,' he said, smiling. 'Cathy's told me so much about you.'

Hannah held out her hand and, as his fingers closed around her own, had to look away in confusion, frantically trying to hide the effect his touch had on her. But he had of course, known. After that first meeting, Hannah went out of her way to avoid the happy couple altogether. Puzzled, Cathy tried to include her in some of their outings and occasionally Hannah went along, but it was too fraught. No matter how she tried, her gaze would stray to Michael, her pulse would race and when once or twice his eyes met her own, unspoken but perfectly understood messages passed between them. Night after night, all those years ago, she would cry herself to sleep feeling that her heart would break.

She was still holding the photograph in her hand when Cathy returned with the coffee.

'Please tell me that you're happy?' Hannah's voice was quiet. She looked at the other girl, searching her eyes for the truth.

'Yes, I am, very happy. And you?' Cathy's tone was challenging, her gaze holding that of her former friend.

Hannah didn't answer. And then she said, 'Cathy? Do you think you'll ever be able to forgive me?'

Cathy handed her a mug and sat down on the sofa before answering. 'I can't say it was easy.' Her voice was tight. Then she added, 'But eventually I managed it. Quite some time ago actually.'

Stunned, Hannah stared at her. 'Then why didn't you get in touch?'

Cathy raised her eyebrows in the gesture Hannah remembered so well. 'Because the first move had to come from you, surely you can see that.'

Hannah looked down. Cathy had always been the clever one.

'You're right,' she said. 'You nearly always were. But first I had to forgive myself.'

There was a moment's silence and then Cathy said, 'And have you? Is that why you've come?'

Hannah searched for the right words. 'I think so. All I know is that I need your friendship as much as ever.'

'And Michael?' Cathy's voice suddenly had an edge.

'He's fine,' Hannah said. 'We're hoping soon to start a family.'

There was a pause. Then Cathy smiled, a broad genuine smile. 'I'm glad,' she said, 'really glad.' She glanced over at the photograph. 'After all, if it hadn't been for you, I'd never have met and married James. What do you think of him?'

'He's absolutely devastating,' Hannah murmured. She put a hand to her mouth as she suddenly realised what she'd just said, but Cathy was laughing so hard she was bent double, with tears running down her cheeks.

'Oh, Han . . .' she gasped, 'welcome back!'

A PERSONAL CHOICE

Brona glanced briefly at her watch. All her careful arrangements were going according to plan, which was a miracle when you considered the one added unpredictable ingredient. She was used to working to a strict deadline, but today was different. As far as she was concerned this event was the most important she'd ever organised, and she desperately wanted it to be a success. Also, there were people coming she needed to impress, some of them strangers, yet they were people who would continue to be an important part of her life for a very long time.

Right, she thought. I'm on top of everything. I've showered, blow-dried my hair, got my makeup on. There's just time for a coffee. But her perfectionist nature wouldn't allow her to leave a bedroom in chaos, and so she spent a precious five minutes restoring it to its normal order.

She hadn't heard the second post being delivered, so was surprised to see the airmail envelope lying tantalisingly on the doormat. She ran quickly down the stairs, but after scanning the familiar handwriting, Brona reluctantly stuffed it in her pocket. Tempted though she was, the letter would have to wait. Coffee was essential, at least the caffeine was, but she couldn't afford to be distracted, not yet.

Half an hour later, having double-checked every detail, she looked around and gave a huge sigh of relief. The food was organised, the flowers were perfect, everything was running to schedule. Going upstairs again, Brona glanced with pride at the suit hanging on her wardrobe door. Grey, with a long jacket, short skirt and crisp white shirt, it was the perfect outfit.

Now, she thought, before I get dressed, I've just got time to read that letter. I'm dying to see what Sarah's got to say.

Ripping open the envelope, it took her only a few minutes to read the familiar scrawl, then she sat with the two sheets of paper in her lap, deep in thought.

Sarah. Her best friend, for many years her only real friend. Was it ten or twelve years since they'd first met?

With the sun pouring through the windows, Brona allowed her mind to roam back to that first meeting all those years ago. She'd gone to the wine bar that evening with some girls from the office, having agreed to accompany them with some reluctance. But her initial protests that she wanted to work on an assignment had met with derision.

'All work and no play, Brona,' they'd teased, and kept it up unmercifully, and so for the sake of a quiet life she'd given in. She'd noticed Sarah, simply yet elegantly dressed in black, immediately, but as she was there with her current boyfriend, they'd merely exchanged smiles. But later in the evening, after he'd disappeared to prop up the bar, Sarah had wandered over to her table, and she and the dark-haired girl had hit it off immediately. Yet it transpired they were very different both in appearance and in their outlook on life. Sarah, quiet and serious, was a foil to Brona's sleek blonde looks, and forceful personality. She'd been deeply impressed that at twenty-three, Brona was already a manager in her department.

'I'm not ambitious at all,' she confided. 'I'm quite happy as I am. I like being a receptionist at the local health centre. I'm not bothered about a high-powered career.'

'But how do you see your future?' Brona, who spent endless hours with her colleagues discussing the many options now open to women, was not only curious but mystified.

'I just want the simple things,' Sarah shrugged. 'I'd like to get married, and have a home and family.'

'Oh, perhaps,' Brona said impatiently. 'But surely you want a life of your own first?'

'Not really,' Sarah murmured with a quiet smile.

Yet despite their opposing outlooks, the two girls had sustained their friendship. Brona had been the one Sarah turned to when a long-term relationship failed. Then a couple of years later, when Brona was made redundant, it was Sarah's support which helped to restore her self confidence.

'We must never drift apart,' Sarah declared, and Brona agreed. Even when Sarah fell in love, married and eventually emigrated to Australia, the two girls wrote regularly. In the meantime, Brona worked hard to fulfil her ambitions, not minding the long hours and increased responsibility, and over the years steadily climbed the promotion ladder.

She smiled ruefully, recalling the one and only time she'd flown out on a three-week visit to Sarah. Although she lived in a pleasant suburb, the huge contrast in their lifestyles had appalled her. Not for her friend the latest fashions, the meals in expensive restaurants, the holidays abroad. With two small children under five and a limited budget, her meagre wardrobe seemed to consist entirely of leggings and teeshirts. As for meals out and travel, "only in my dreams," Sarah had joked.

Yet she'd seemed so happy, leaving Brona completely bewildered. Oh, the children were lovely, of course, but Brona just couldn't understand how anyone could sacrifice their whole life to them. After all, what had women fought for these past years, if it wasn't to be freed from the drudgery of domesticity?

'You'll understand, one day,' Sarah said. 'I don't need the challenge of a job at the moment. You thrive on it, you love the smart clothes, the busy cut and thrust. I'm happy as I am, honestly.'

Brona glanced down at the letter again. Sarah had written to say that she had decided to go back to work. She was planning to study, to enrol on a computer course at a nearby college.

'I am, at last, filled with ambition,' she wrote. 'There are lots of opportunities here if you have the skills. I know you'll be surprised after all I've said, but I feel differently now that the children are at school. Perhaps life is like that, nothing remains constant. Pete is being very supportive, and we could certainly use some extra money. But I think it's seeing how successful and single-minded you've been which has spurred me on. Even now, when your life is about to change, you are still full of determination.'

Brona gave a wry smile, imagining Sarah's look of amazement when she received and read the letter she'd written the day before. Would her own unexpected decision surprise her friend?

Startled out of her reverie by the insistent ring of the phone, Brona got up and went to pick up the extension.

'Yes, everything's fine,' she said reassuringly, as she heard the familiar brisk voice. 'Don't worry if you can't get here until the last minute, I'm completely in control.'

Glancing at her watch, she realised with a shock that it was time she was dressed, but with her accustomed efficiency, within a few minutes she was ready. Sarah's letter she propped up by the side of her bed ready to answer later, and then she stood thoughtfully in front of the gilt full length mirror. Turning sideways she checked the fit of the tailored skirt, loving the silky feel of the sheer expensive tights. Her gold earrings matched exactly the gold pendant around her neck, and she knew she had never looked better. Brona gazed intently at her reflection, seeing a softer look in her eyes, a bloom on her cheeks. Yes, she was satisfied with her appearance, proud of it even. So many times she'd organised an important function, but never one with such pride.

Then, with a gentle smile, Brona crossed over to the other side of the large, airy room. There, fitting snugly into a corner was a pretty blue canopied crib. Tenderly, carefully, she lifted out her baby son. If there was one thing in life of which she was certain, it was that this soft, warm bundle had brought her more love and joy than she'd ever thought possible.

With his downy head nestling into her shoulder, Brona carefully placed a lacy shawl around her child, and said softly. 'Are you ready to meet your relatives, little one? The whole family is coming to your christening.' She paused as she heard a car pull up in the drive, and carried him over to the window. Peering out, she pulled the net curtain aside, and then waved. 'It's your Daddy,' she said. 'He's just in time.'

Brona walked to the bedroom door, and looked back at the airmail letter. 'You were right, Sarah.' she murmured."Now, at last I understand. But while I wish you all the luck in the world with your new career, I've made my own decision. I know what I want to do.'

She looked down with a loving smile. 'While you're so small,' she whispered to the sleeping baby, 'I'm going to stay at home with you!'

KINDRED SPIRITS

'Don't look at me like that!' Zoe glared into the glowing amber eyes of the black cat sitting in the doorway of her bedroom. 'Honestly, you're more disapproving than my Dad used to be.' She turned over, snuggling down beneath the duvet. Last night had been great despite her hangover, and she thought wistfully of the tall, dark-haired guy she'd met at the bar the previous evening. Or rather she had exchanged glances with. He had been sitting with a group of friends and she'd first noticed him when, as she casually glanced over, their gaze met and he'd raised his glass in acknowledgement. And then it had become a sort of game, he would raise his eyebrows, his eyes full of laughter and she would smile back. Her two girlfriends teased her, saying that he was just a flirt who was probably off the leash. But all too soon, it had been time to leave the bar to go to a colleague's party and Lisa had become impatient. 'Come on, you two, we'll be in his bad books if we're late.' As they rose, Zoe glanced over her shoulder at the far table, only to find her view obscured by a newly arrived couple standing in front of it.

And so, she thought, eventually swinging her legs out of bed and wincing at the twinge of pain in her head, that's another possible romance biting the dust. She'd really fancied him as well. She padded across the pink carpet in her bare feet, which was hardly the colour for an up and coming journalist, but already there when she moved in. Now, she now rather liked it.

Felix was nowhere to be seen, probably in the kitchen sulking she thought. Honestly, he was a strange cat, happy enough to curl up with her if she was ill, but let her come home with a hangover and it was a different matter. Going into the tiny bathroom she reached for her toothbrush and then seeing her reflection in the bathroom mirror grimaced. It wasn't surprising that Felix was freaked out, her blonde streaked hair was standing up like Jedward! Right, it would have to be straight into the shower before opening a tin of his favourite cat food, maybe then they would be friends again.

Half an hour later, Zoe was munching wholemeal toast and honey in the hope that it would sort out her headache. A mug of strong coffee was at her side. She watched Felix eating, as always impressed by the delicate way he would pick up a morsel before moving on to another. He had better table manners than some people, and with that thought an image of her previous boyfriend popped into her mind. Rob had loved his food and been prone to shovelling forkfuls into his mouth. He hadn't been averse to talking with his mouth full, either.

'Now, you wouldn't do that, would you sweetie?' Felix didn't even glance up, so intent was he. He had come to live with her after her beloved Gran went into a nursing home where much to the family's relief, she was happy and well cared for. And during the discussion that followed about her cat, Zoe had seen everyone's gaze turn to her.

'Think how lovely it would be Zoe, to come home to a welcome,' her mum said.

She'd been reluctant at first, but within a couple

of weeks Felix had become a central part of her life. Something, she thought grimly, that Rob had never understood, as was proved in one fateful scene. Wanting to watch Match of the Day and unaware that Zoe had come to the doorway, Rob had found Felix snoozing in the armchair which had the best view of the TV. With a muttered expletive, Rob had thrown him off then roughly kicked him aside with the toe of his shoe. Back arched Felix had stalked away leaving Zoe seething. Whose home was it anyway, her boyfriend's or her pet's? Thankful that she'd resisted Rob's suggestion that he move in, Zoe had promptly dumped him. It wasn't only a case of 'love me, love my cat,' she'd seen a side of him she didn't like. Why would she want to be with someone like that?

With Zoe finding that the memory of the guy she'd seen in the wine bar remained with her, finally her friends got fed up. 'Oh, for heaven's sake, let's go back there,' Lisa said. 'I'm telling you though, it's a waste of time. I can pick a loser a mile off.'

Zoe bit back a biting comment about Lisa's last boyfriend, whose freedom was now restricted by the courts, and they did go to the wine bar and as she half-expected, he wasn't there. But Zoe was a determined Taurus and a few days later, she went alone. And there he was before the bar, tall, dark and gazing reflectively into an empty wine glass. She stood a small distance along from him and waited. He glanced her way, and she saw his eyes light up with pleasure. 'Hello there. I was hoping . . .'

Smiling at him she said, 'So was I.'

He bought them both wine, and after exchanging names they went over to a corner table, teasing how they had first noticed each other. Zoe found herself more attracted to him with every minute, and conversation flowed over replenished glasses until, 'Another?' James offered, after their third.

'I'd better not. Felix, that's my cat, hates me with a hangover.'

He grinned. 'You must have been grumpy with him one time, they're judgmental are cats.'

She laughed. 'You sound as if you have one yourself.'

'I do, she's called Missy.' He hesitated. 'Do you reckon they might like each other?'

Zoe's gaze held his. 'We could always find out.'

⌒

NOTHING TO PROVE

It hit her as soon as she opened her eyes. It was Friday, and what was happening on Friday? Sara was arriving from America, that's what! The saintly Sara, the divine Sara, the one who made Tom's eyes sparkle at the very mention of her name.

'Wait until you meet her, Jackie,' he'd been enthusing all week. 'You two are going to be great pals.'

Oh, yeah? thought Jackie grimly. With my husband's old girlfriend? I mean, what planet is he on?

Her friends had been stunned when she told them Tom had invited Sara to stay with them for a few days.

'Just until she gets herself sorted out,' he explained airily, too full of excited anticipation to notice the look of horror on Jackie's face.

Now let's get this straight, thought Jackie, as she closed her eyes in an attempt to shut out the impending day of doom. It's not that I'm jealous! She was confident enough of Tom's love not to feel insecure just because a past girlfriend showed up. After all, if he'd wanted her he'd have married her, wouldn't he? No, if she was really honest with herself, she was just sick of having Sara's virtues thrust down her throat, not just by Tom, but by his mother!

'Lovely girl, she was,' she confided to Jackie when they first met. 'I always had great hopes for Sara and Tom. She was a fantastic cook, you know. And she could sew, she made these curtains for me.' She sighed. 'Still, you can't choose for them, can you?'

Jackie, whose idea of cooking was sticking something ready-made in the microwave, and avoided even threading a needle if she could help it, gritted her teeth and kept quiet.

Later though, she moaned to her friends. 'I ask you, in this day and age. She sounds like Doris Day, the second. Well, if Tom's looking for someone who'll have his slippers by the fire and a pinny on when he comes home, he's shopping at the wrong store.'

But Tom continued shopping, blithely disregarding his mother's list of Jackie's shortcomings and three weeks ago, they were married. He ate takeaways with gusto, never even noticed the ready-made curtains, and seemed more than content to live in cheerful chaos.

No, it wasn't that she was jealous at all! Jackie furrowed her brow, trying to analyse just how she did feel. It was that she wanted to prove something, not to Tom, she didn't need to, he loved her for what she was. Not to his mother, either, though a few Brownie points wouldn't go amiss there! No, Jackie wanted to prove her own abilities. She hated to think there were skills she couldn't master. Not nuclear science of course, she wasn't daft, but normal skills like proper cooking shouldn't be beyond her, surely? She could see the point to that, she liked her food as much as the next person.

But Sara was arriving from America now, today, and Jackie still hadn't practised. But, with her usual optimism, she didn't see a problem. Okay, she hadn't got a cookery book, but she watched the telly didn't she, even if she'd only seen the end of one programme. Anyway, there were loads of recipes on the internet.

But the time she'd shopped on the way home from work, and tidied up, Jackie was racing against time. Tom, of course, was meeting Sara at the airport. 'It's the least I can do,' he insisted. 'Her parents were always so good to me.'

Jackie had decided on chicken, just in case Sara wasn't into red meat. If she's a vegetarian, I'll kill her, she muttered, then grinned at her own joke! But when she peeked in the oven at the skinless chicken portions, they looked like something from the Sahara desert. Frantically, she cast around, then found the packet of sauce lurking under a tea towel where she'd dropped it when the phone rang. Sara poured it over the chicken and then shoved the dish back in the oven with a sigh of relief. That should do the trick. New potatoes and frozen garden peas, plus an M & S gateau for dessert, what could be easier?

And then Tom sent her a text to say that Sara's plane was delayed, and too late Jackie realised that she should have allowed for that. Rushing into the kitchen she turned down the oven, but eventually the previously plump chicken portions shrank into pathetic dried lumps and as for the sauce . . . the aroma in the kitchen left much to be desired. It took Jackie five minutes to chuck the chicken in the bin, open the windows, and spray air freshener. Then she did some serious thinking.

What the hell was she doing, trying to be someone she wasn't? For deep down, Jackie knew she'd been trying to impress Sara, knew she resented the fact that the other girl might be more capable than herself. Well, so what! She was happy, wasn't she? Tom was mad about her, even his Mum was thawing out. If she did decide to take up cooking, she'd do it in her own time, perhaps enrol on a course. To be honest, even she was getting fed up of pizzas. And if Tom wanted her and Sara to be friends, then Jackie was up for it.

So Jackie did what she normally did on a Friday night. Decided they could all have a takeaway, chose a DVD and switched on the TV.

When Tom eventually burst through the door, carrying luggage, Jackie rose from the sofa to see him followed by a slim, attractive redhead. 'Hi, you must be Jackie.'

She moved forward and kissed her lightly on the cheek. 'Lovely to meet you. But you must be starving.' Jackie glanced at Tom. 'I'd intended to cook something but somehow . . .'

'That's brilliant,' Sara said with delight. 'Because I've been dying to have English fish and chips again. Is there a chippy nearby, would that be okay?'

Tom grinned at Jackie. 'Suit me, I'll go and fetch some.'

'Meanwhile,' Jackie said, with a wide smile. 'I'll make you a decent cup of tea.' Because that, Jackie thought was one thing she did perfectly.

DRIVING MRS MURPHY

Angie watched the old lady walk awkwardly down the steps of the courthouse and successfully negotiate the safety of the level pavement before straightening and peering around her.

Angie lowered the cab window. 'Mrs Murphy?'

'Yes, dear, I'm so glad you're on time. Your husband was too, when he picked me up.'

'We do our best.' Angie opened the cab door and settled her inside.

Checking her mirror, she expertly steered the car away from the crowded street and glanced at her watch. Plenty of time to drop off her fare, then that was her shift finished for the day. It was ages since she and Steve had managed a night out, and she didn't want him to be in a bad mood by being late.

Angie frowned. There she went again, anticipating trouble. Okay, so Steve was a bit short-tempered these days, but then so was she. Pressure of work, that was the reason. Building up their own mini-cab business hadn't been easy, and now they were expanding with more drivers, the problems seemed to multiply.

'Are you all right, dear? You look worried.'

Angie had almost forgotten Mrs Murphy in the passenger seat.

'Yes love, fine.What have you been up to then, armed robbery?'

'Oh, nothing like that. No, I like to go in the public gallery, it makes a change from the telly.'

A few minutes later Angie drew the gleaming cab to a halt outside a small terraced house. 'There you are,' she said. 'And as you're my last fare for today, I'm off home for a cup of tea.'

Mrs Murphy looked hopefully at her. 'You wouldn't like to have one with me, would you?'

Angie sensed the loneliness behind the faded blue eyes, and inwardly sighing said, 'Thank you, but I mustn't be long.'

The old lady's face lit up. 'I'll have the kettle on in a trice.'

Angie followed her into a neat sitting room. It seemed somehow bare of personal touches, just one photograph of a moustached middle-aged man, and a few ornaments on the tiled fireplace. As she sat in the silence, Angie couldn't help thinking about Steve's tension that morning. She didn't know what was wrong with him. The business was going well, it was hard work but neither of them minded that. They'd expected it, that was one reason they'd agreed not to have children. Only they didn't seem to talk any more, not properly. It was all surface stuff, the day's happenings, the weather, trivial gossip. Angie missed sharing her feelings, her dreams, her problems.

'Here we are,' Mrs Murphy bustled in.

Angie looked at the prettily set tray, with a china teapot, milk jug and sugar bowl, all on an embroidered cloth. She thought of her own tea ritual with thick mugs, dripping teabags and milk straight from the bottle. This was nice, soothing somehow. The finer things of life, she thought, they do make a difference. I ought to make more of an effort.

'Do you live on your own?' she asked.

'Yes, I've been widowed over 20 years,' she nodded at the photograph. 'That was my husband.'

Angie took a biscuit and sipped her tea. 'Have you a family?' Somehow she knew the answer already. Where were the proud photos of children and grandchildren?

A shadow passed over the old lady's face. 'No,' she said. 'And never a day goes by that I don't regret it.'

'I'm sorry,' Angie said awkwardly. 'It was by choice, then?'

Mrs Murphy put down her cup. 'Well, it was and it wasn't …' She stared into the distance, and said quietly, 'We didn't talk, you see, didn't communicate. People didn't so much in those days, even husbands and wives. Jack didn't seem to like children, hadn't got much patience with them. At least that's how it seemed when we first met. And he knew how much I loved my work – I was a nurse, you know.'

She brought her gaze back to Angie. 'Somehow life gets so busy and time passes. It was only when it was too late that Jack admitted that his one regret was that that he hadn't had a son or a daughter. Only he loved me too much to ask me to give up my career.'

'And you?' Angie asked, every nerve in her body straining to hear the answer.

'All I wanted was to make Jack happy,' she said. 'The problem was that women of my generation were brought up to think of others, never of themselves. So he never knew how I really felt, how much I would have liked a family. It seems so stupid now that we didn't talk about it. But he was a good man, I was very lucky.'

Angie stared at her, numbed by the impact of her words. It was weird, pure chance that she was listening to this conversation.

That evening, she looked anxiously at Steve. Dependable he may be, but was he going to understand? Should she tell him how she felt, how she'd changed? But time was passing, and she could wait forever for exactly the right moment. It wasn't enough to have courage, one should act upon it. 'Steve,' she faltered, then the question came out in a rush. 'Are you sure you don't want children?' In an agony of suspense, she waited for his answer.

He gave a hesitant look, not the swift and defensive reply she'd expected. 'I thought you wanted to concentrate on the business.'

'I did, I still think that's important but … oh, Steve, I want a baby so much,' she confessed.

He gazed at her for one long moment, and then he smiled. 'Angie, I can't tell you how happy I am to hear you say that. I wouldn't have thought it at one time, but I feel the same.'

Much later, they lay talking into the night and vowed never again to hide their feelings from each other. Honesty and communication was vital in any relationship, and for that wisdom Angie knew she had to thank one sweet old lady.

'Steve,' she murmured. 'If we have a little boy, I think I'd like to call him Jack.'

'Great,' he said sleepily. 'And if it's a girl?'

Angie smiled to herself. She could hardly call her Mrs Murphy, so …

'I'll tell you after I've seen a new friend of mine.'

A FATEFUL MEETING

'The train arriving at Platform 2 is
the 6.35 from Manchester . . .'

The tannoy's announcement caused people to move forward on the platform, but Olivia hung back, standing alone, a little apart. With her dark hair blowing in the breeze, her tall slim figure attracted many an admiring glance, but she was unaware of the interest she aroused. She was totally focused, waiting with impatience to meet Luke. He was such a major part of her life, she could hardly believe she'd only known him for three months.

'I'm glad I don't have to do long-distance jobs too often,' he'd grinned, soon after he arrived to work on the extension to the firm's offices. 'It's bad enough during the week, but I couldn't stand being away at weekends.'

Olivia, who'd been dying for a chance to chat to the dark, good-looking site manager, had felt her heart sink. He was married – she knew it, either that or involved in a relationship. No man so attractive could possibly be single, she just wasn't that lucky.

'Any particular reason?' she asked tentatively.

'I've got a four year old boy.' He glanced at her, and then said quietly, 'My wife died, three years ago.'

'Oh, I'm so sorry. Who takes care of him during the week?'

'When I'm working away? My parents, but as you

can imagine, I miss him.'

Then he'd smiled, and carried on with his work. But later that day, when she left the premises, he was waiting.

'I wondered,' he said, 'whether you'd care to come out for a drink? That is, if I'm not stepping on anyone's toes.'

She'd smiled and shaken her head, and after that they became inseparable. During the week, they would go out for a drink, a meal, occasionally to the cinema or theatre. But often, they were content to spend the evening in Olivia's small flat, talking, watching TV, listening to music. Except for weekends.

Then, when the building work was finished, Luke returned home.

Friends scoffed, saying that would be the last she saw of him, but Olivia ignored them. She had no doubts because she was confident that what she and Luke had come to share was special.

Now, after a month, four long weeks without seeing him and suffering complacent looks, she was about to prove them wrong. For Luke had rung to say he was coming to see her. It had been arranged before, but each time he'd had to postpone the visit. Once it had been because he had to work, then his little boy had gone down with chickenpox.

'He's a bit fretful – I don't feel I can leave him,' he'd said. 'I know you'll understand.' Now, as at last the train began to draw into the station, Olivia's excitement and anticipation grew. She couldn't wait to see him, the past weeks had been so lonely, it had seemed an eternity.

But several minutes later she was still standing alone.

With bewilderment and bitter disappointment, she watched the guard slam the last carriage door and blow his whistle. Where was Luke? Why on earth wasn't he on the train? Hurriedly, she rummaged in her bag to find her mobile phone and rang him. But there was no connection. Luke wouldn't tell her he was coming, and then just not turn up, he wouldn't! What had he said before he left?

'I love you, Olivia. Trust me, I'll never let you down!'

He'd been so anxious to reassure her, knowing of her unhappy and confused childhood. How lonely she'd been, how she'd always longed to be part of a real family.

'I'll make your dream come true, I promise.'

Held close in his arms, she'd believed him.

Now, she stood uncertainly on the cold platform. He must have missed it, what other explanation could there be? It began to rain, and checking the time of the next train, she headed for the comfort of the brightly-lit coffee bar.

Waiting at the counter, she glanced around the crowded room, her attention caught by a young girl huddled in a corner. Her face pinched with weariness, she couldn't have been more than fourteen. Olivia saw her tense and dart a frightened glance at the door as it opened. Then she looked down, struggling against tears.

Thoughtfully, Olivia paid for her coffee, and after some hesitation went over to the table where the girl was sitting and said, 'Do you mind if I sit here?'

The girl shrugged. As Olivia sat down and put her polystyrene cup on the table, she asked gently, 'Are you okay?'

In utter misery, the girl shook her head.

Olivia hesitated, then said, 'Tell me to mind my own business if you like…'

The girl looked up warily.

'Are you running away?'

'What's it got to do with you?' The girl's voice was sharp, but it was obvious that Olivia's question had hit home.

'Let's just say I've been there, and believe me, it can be as bad or even worse than anything you're leaving behind.'

'You don't know anything about me,' the girl said defiantly.

'With me,' Olivia continued, 'it was because I was sick of being pushed around. I'd lived in children's homes all my life. Then one day, I had this romantic notion that I was old enough to look after myself.' Watching the girl carefully, she saw a flicker of interest in her pale blue eyes.

'What happened?'

Olivia shuddered at the memory. 'I ended up sleeping on the streets. When they found me, I was dirty, frightened and hadn't eaten for two days.' She took three coins out of her purse. 'Why don't you get yourself another drink?'

As she went to the counter, Olivia's heart went out to her. The slump of those thin shoulders, the vulnerable bravado, it was like looking at herself all those years ago.

The girl returned with a Coke. 'It must have been awful,' she said, 'not having a family, I mean.'

'It was something I wanted more than anything in the world. It still is,' Olivia told her.

'Mum's okay,' the girl said, 'it's my Dad, he's always

on at me.' She twisted a strand of fair hair around her fingers. 'We had this dreadful row. I don't stay out that late, only the same as my friends, but he went on as if I was a criminal!'

'He's probably just trying to protect you. I wish I'd had someone like that. When I think what could have happened to me out there on my own, you must know the dangers. Why don't you go back home, try to sort things out?' Olivia suggested. She watched the indecision in the girl's eyes.

'Do you think they'll be mad?'

'More likely relieved.' Olivia passed over her mobile.

'It's okay, I've got mine.' She looked up sheepishly. 'I'd switched it off.'

Not until she knew the girl's parents were coming to collect her in ten minutes, did Olivia go back to wait on the chilly platform. Fleetingly, she wondered whether it was true that life was all chance? If Luke had been on that train, she wouldn't have been there to help that kid, and who knew what might have happened.

Through the now driving rain, the expected train drew into the station. Patiently at first, then with increasing panic, Olivia searched the stream of passengers but to no avail. There was no sign of him. With a sob choking her throat, a feeling of despair swept over her. No . . . her mind, her heart refused to believe it. Her friends were wrong. Luke couldn't have been using her just as a distraction while working away from home. He loved her, she couldn't have been mistaken!

The guard began to slam the doors, and in despair Olivia turned and began to walk slowly, unsteadily, away.

'Olivia!'

Swiftly she turned, to see Luke struggling with a carriage door at the far end of the train. It had jammed, and a guard went to assist. A few seconds later, he was lifting down a child, and facing her, his arms wide and welcoming.

With happiness and relief flooding through her, Olivia ran to him.

'We were stuck in a traffic jam,' he explained, 'so we missed our train. I couldn't phone because with brilliant timing my mobile's packed in.'

'Never mind, you're here now!' Olivia didn't care what had happened, he was here, he was smiling at her, everything was going to be all right.

'You weren't worried, were you? You knew I'd come?'

'Of course I did! Anyway, I think it was fate!' At his puzzled look, she whispered, 'I'll tell you later.'

She looked down at the small boy standing shyly at his side.

Luke moved him forward. 'Sean, this is Olivia.'

'Hi, Sean,' Olivia said gently. 'Your daddy's told me lots about you.'

Anxious brown eyes looked into hers. 'He's told me lots about you, too.'

She laughed. Raising her head, Olivia searched the platform, breathing a sigh of relief as she saw the young girl leaving with her parents. With her father's arm protectively around her shoulders, she turned and waved.

She's going home with her family, Olivia thought. And I'm going home with mine. With shining eyes, she waited as Luke picked up his bags. Then with Sean between them, his hands clasped in theirs, the three of them walked out of the station.

Margaret Kaine is also a successful romantic novelist.

She has written seven sagas set in The Potteries, UK

RING OF CLAY
(which won two literary prizes)

ROSEMARY
(a sequel to Ring of Clay but stands alone)

A GIRL OF HER TIME

FRIENDS & FAMILIES

ROSES FOR REBECCA

RIBBON OF MOONLIGHT

SONG FOR A BUTTERFLY

also
DANGEROUS DECISIONS
a romantic suspense set in the Edwardian era

All are available in Paperback, Large Print and Audio
CD and, of course as ebooks

More information about Margaret and her books can
be found on her website
www.margaretkaine.com
Why not follow her on Facebook, Twitter, Pinterest
and Instagram

Lightning Source UK Ltd.
Milton Keynes UK
UKHW02f1221081117
312337UK00007B/375/P